For Emily and Giles Woolley

First published 1985 by Walker Books Ltd
87 Vauxhall Walk, London SE11 5HJ

This edition published 2009

2 4 6 8 10 9 7 5 3 1

This book has been typeset in Garamond Educational

Printed in China

British Library Cataloguing in Publication Data:
a catalogue record for this book is available from the British Library.

ISBN 978-0-7445-2644-8

www.walker.co.uk

Noisy

Shirley Hughes

WALKER BOOKS
AND SUBSIDIARIES

LONDON • BOSTON • SYDNEY • AUCKLAND

Noisy noises!
Pan lids clashing,

Dog barking,
Plate smashing,

Telephone ringing,
Baby bawling,

Midnight cats
Cat-a-wauling,

Door slamming,

Aeroplane zooming,

Vacuum cleaner
Vroom-vroom-vrooming,

And if I dance and sing a tune,
Baby joins in with a saucepan and spoon.

Gentle noises…
Dry leaves swishing,

Falling rain,
Splashing, splishing,

Rustling trees,
Hardly stirring,

Lazy cat
Softly purring.

Story's over,
Bedtime's come,

Crooning baby
Sucks his thumb.

All quiet, not a peep,

Everyone is fast asleep.